ABDO Publishing Company is the exclusive school and library distributor of Rabbit Ears Books.

Library bound edition 2007.

Copyright © 1995 Rabbit Ears Entertainment, LLC.,
S. Norwalk, Connecticut.

Library of Congress Cataloging-in-Publication Data

MacHale, D. J.
    East of the sun, west of the moon / written by D.J. MacHale ; illustrated by Vivienne Flesher.
        p. cm.
    Summary: A girl travels east of the sun and west of the moon to free her beloved prince
from a magic spell.
    ISBN-13: 978-1-59961-306-2
    ISBN-10: 1-59961-306-9
    [1. Fairy tales. 2. Folklore—Norway.] I. Flesher, Vivienne, ill. II. Title.

PZ8.M17628Eas 2006
398.209481'02—dc22
[E]

                                                                2006042592

All Rabbit Ears books are reinforced library binding
and manufactured in the United States of America.

EAST WEST OF OF THE THE SUN MOON

WRITTEN BY D. J. MACHALE   ILLUSTRATED BY VIVIENNE FLESHER

RABBIT EARS BOOKS

Hidden deep in the blue forest of Norway, in a tiny hut, there lived a peasant farmer and his family. ☽ His children were pretty to the last, but none prettier than his youngest daughter. Her long golden hair and radiant smile brought light to the darkest of days, for she didn't care that they were poor, only that they were happy.

☽ One evening, late in the fall of that year, the sky grew cloudy and dark. A fierce storm lashed the small hut, making the walls creak and groan. The peasant family sat huddled by the fire, when there came three heavy raps on the door. ☽ "Who would be out on such a beastly night?" exclaimed the father as he opened the door.

He then found himself staring up at a great white bear. "Good evening," said the giant bear. ☽ "Good evening to you," replied the peasant. ☽ "I bring you a proposal. If you give me your youngest daughter, I will make you as rich as you are now poor, and she will live with me as a princess." ☽ Now the man truly liked the idea of being rich, so he brought the proposal to his daughter. ☽ "We will be rich, and you will live as a princess! All you

have to do is live with this handsome white bear." ☽ The girl thought of her family and of the great fortune they would have if she would go to live with the bear. But she was greatly saddened that her father would choose riches over the company of his youngest daughter. Still, she would live with the white bear for her family's sake. ☽ And so the beautiful young girl packed her ragged clothes into a bundle and sadly said good-bye to her family.

nce she was outside, the bear turned to her. ☽ "Are you afraid?" he asked. ☽ The girl trembled with fear, but shook her head, no. ☽ "Then hold on tightly to my coat." ☽ The girl climbed up onto the back of the huge beast, and off they went. ☽ They traveled a long, long way through the dark forest until they came to the base of a steep mountain. The white bear scraped at the ground before a large boulder. At once it rolled aside to reveal a vast golden cavern. ☽ Inside the magnificent cave, they came to a gigantic table laden with food

and drink. It was more food than the girl had seen in her lifetime. ☽ The white bear then gave her a tiny silver bell. He instructed her that when she wanted anything, she was to ring it and she would have what she wanted at once. The bear then left her to her lonely feast. ☽ When she had eaten her fill, she grew sleepy. No sooner did she touch the bell than she found herself in a magnificent golden bed, with silk pillows and curtains of the richest tapestry. It was truly fit for a princess. So the girl lay down and was soon fast asleep.

Later that night, when all was quiet and still, the girl was awakened by someone who had lain down beside her. She became rigid with fear, for she didn't know if this person meant her harm, and it was so dark she couldn't see who it was. But the mysterious person didn't even touch her. He slept peacefully, without making a sound. And when the light of dawn crept in through the window, he was gone. ☽ When the bear awoke her, she asked him who the mysterious visitor was, but the bear gruffly told her she had only been dreaming.

☽ As the days passed, the girl spent much time with the white bear. He was kind and thoughtful, and in time, their friendship grew. But every night the mysterious visitor came in the dark and slept beside her, only to be gone by morning.

ow, the girl had everything a princess could possibly want, but after many weeks she grew silent and sad. ☽ When the bear asked what was troubling her, she answered: ☽ "I haven't seen my family in such a long time. I'm terribly homesick." ☽ The white bear didn't like to see the girl so unhappy. "I will bring you to visit your family for one day," he said, "but you must promise me one thing. You must never talk of your life here with me. Even if your own mother asks you, you must say nothing." ☽ The girl eagerly assented to do as he asked. The white bear then announced that they

would set off immediately. The girl was overjoyed. She quickly leapt up onto the bear's back, and off they trundled on the long journey back through the woods to the home of her family. ☽ The bear brought the girl to a clearing in the woods where her family's cottage once had been, but in its place there now stood a magnificent white house. The sight of it made the girl's spirits soar, for the bear had kept his promise and her family was now as rich as they were once poor. ☽ "Mind what I have told you, or you will make us both unhappy." ☽ With that, the white bear turned and disappeared back into the forest.

The girl's family had everything they ever wanted now and were very happy. The young girl wished they had missed her more, but she was pleased to see them so content. ☽ Later, after they had finished a sumptuous feast, the girl's mother took her aside and asked her about her life with the bear. The girl remembered her solemn promise to the bear, and refused, but her mother grew angry and insisted, and finally, the girl relented. ☽ She told her mother how every night as soon as she put out the light, a stranger came and lay down beside her, and

how she never saw him because he was always up and away before morning. ☽ "The white bear is very nice," she said, "but there are no other people in the cavern. All day long I walk about alone. Maybe this stranger would keep me company. I wish I could see him."

On hearing this, her mother became quite anxious. ☽ "Oh dear! It may well be the master of all these riches who lies down beside you. I'll give you a bit of candle which you should hide. When he comes at night, burn the candle and you will have light to see him. Perhaps then he will make you his queen and we can live in his castle." ☽ The lonely girl took the candle and hid it in her sleeve, ready to carry out her

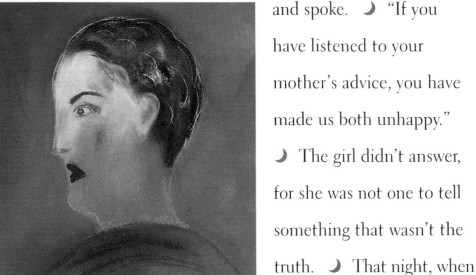

mother's plan. ☽ When the night drew near, the white bear returned and fetched her away. As they traveled, the bear turned to her and spoke. ☽ "If you have listened to your mother's advice, you have made us both unhappy." ☽ The girl didn't answer, for she was not one to tell something that wasn't the truth. ☽ That night, when she had gone to bed, again the mysterious stranger came and lay down beside her.

When she heard that he slept, she got up and lit the candle. ☽ When the light shone across the stranger, the girl saw the most handsome prince that anyone could imagine. He was so handsome, and sleeping so peacefully, that the young girl couldn't resist leaning down and kissing him. And so she did. ☽ But as she kissed him, three drops of hot tallow fell from the candle and dripped on his white silken shirt. The prince awoke with a start. ☽ "What have you done?" he said. "I warned you not to listen to your mother!"

☽ The young girl didn't understand, for it was the white bear who had given her the warning, not this handsome prince. ☽ "You

see me now as I once was," said the prince sadly. "The Queen of Trolls has bewitched me so I am a white bear by day and a man by night." ☽ "You?" the girl said. "You are my friend the bear?" ☽ "Yes," he replied. "If I could find someone to love me as a bear, and live with me for one year, the spell would be broken. But now, alas! I must return to her castle and be cursed forever!" The young girl felt ashamed for having broken her promise. ☽ "Tell me the way and I'll come to your rescue." ☽ "Oh, the queen's castle is in a far-off place that lies east of the sun and west of the moon, and you surely will never find your way there."

Then the candle blew out and the prince was gone. ☽ The darkness grew cold and surrounded the girl, and she fell into a deep and troubled sleep. And when she awoke, she found herself lying in the midst of the dense forest. ☽ By her side lay the bundle of rags she had brought with her from home. She wept to think of what she had done. But then, wiping the tears from her eyes, she resolved to find her prince in the castle that lay east of the sun and west of the moon. ☽ The girl struggled for many days to make her way through the dank forest. Finally, just as she

was about to collapse, a gentle breeze floated through the trees and caressed her cheek. It was the East Wind. ☽ "Where are you going?" he asked her with a gentle breath. ☽ "I am searching for the castle that lies east of the sun and west of the moon. Can you help me get there?" ☽ "I would like to," said the East Wind, "but I am nothing more than a breeze. But perhaps my brother the West Wind can carry you there. I will take you to him." ☽ And with that the East Wind wrapped himself around the girl and carried her up above the treetops.

After a while there were no more trees, and the East Wind left the girl on a barren, rocky landscape where the wind seemed to be blowing every which way. ☽ It came from her left, then from her right, then blew straight in her face and made her blink. ☽ A giddy laugh echoed off the mountains, and she knew that she had reached the home of the mischievous West Wind.

☽ "I am searching for the castle that lies east of the sun and west of the moon," she told the West Wind. "Can you help me get there?" ☽ The West Wind laughed again. ☽ "I might and I might not," he said. "It could be this way or that way, or perhaps another way

entirely! There's no telling for sure. It all depends on which way the wind blows. Ha ha ha!"

☽ And with that the West Wind swirled about the girl and turned her around and around and around...and then he knocked her to the ground and blew away. ☽ The girl lay there on the hard ground and wept again, for she had traveled many days and nights, and still she was no closer to finding the castle. But then she thought of the prince in the clutches of the Troll Queen and slowly she picked herself up and started on her journey again. ☽ After she had walked for two days, the girl saw that the land was turning green and the sky was brightening.

The breeze that blew was growing warmer and warmer, and suddenly she realized that she had reached the home of the South Wind.  "I am searching for the castle that lies east of the sun and west of the moon," she told him. "Can you help me get there?"  The South Wind was silent for a long time before he answered.  "I have traveled far in my time here on the earth, but never as far as that. Only my brother the North Wind would have the strength to carry you east of the sun and west of the moon. I will take you to him."  The South Wind picked up the girl and placed her on his back.  "But be warned, child!" he told her. "My brother's great strength is not matched by his manners."

As they journeyed farther and farther still, the sky darkened to blackness and the land below them turned to ice. The air turned bitter cold, and they now felt the breath of the powerful North Wind. ☽ "Blast you!" he said to them. "What do you want?" ☽ The North Wind raged so wildly that icy-cold puffs swirled all about his house, making the girl shiver. ☽ "I am searching for the castle that lies east of the sun and west of the moon," she told him. "Can you help me get there?" ☽ "Once, a long time ago, I blew an aspen leaf there. It tired me so that I couldn't blow a puff for many weeks afterward." ☽ "I am searching for a bewitched prince," the girl explained. "He needs my help." ☽ "Are you the one he wishes to be with?" inquired the North Wind. ☽ "I am," said the girl. Immediately the North Wind swelled with pride and spoke. ☽ "If you are not afraid, I'll take you on my back and blow you there myself." ☽ "Nothing could make me afraid," she replied. "No, no, no matter how wildly you storm, for with all my heart I wish to go there!" ☽ "Very well then!" And with that the North Wind puffed himself up so stout and so big that the girl thought he would burst for sure. ☽ Then, with a great swirl he lifted her high, high up into the air and took her on her way so fast that it seemed they would never stop until they reached the end of the world.

Down below, there was such a storm that houses and long tracts of wood were torn up. When the North Wind swept over the great sea, hundreds of ships were tossed about in the high waves. ☽ On and on they blew over the open sea. Finally the North Wind began to grow weary. The girl noticed that they were so close to the water now that the crests of the waves washed about her heels. ☽ "Are you afraid?" the North

Wind asked. ☽ "No," she answered, "Look! I see land!" ☽ The North Wind had just enough strength left to cast her up onto the shore. She looked up to thank the North Wind for his help, but found herself alone in the soft sand, exhausted and shivering. Through the gray mist, she saw something that made her heart leap. A castle! It was the castle that lay east of the sun and west of the moon. She had found it at last.

She immediately jumped up and ran toward the castle. But when she entered the great hall, she stopped dead in her tracks, for she saw that the entire castle was filled with the frozen trophies of the Troll Queen. ☽ Then a voice bellowed, shaking the castle walls.

☽ "Who dares enter my castle?"

☽ The young girl started and then looked up to see the Troll Queen shamble from behind her grand throne of ice. ☽ Though she was terribly frightened, the young girl stepped forward and spoke: ☽ "I have come for the prince who has been bewitched into a white bear." ☽ On hearing this, the Troll Queen let out a hollow laugh that made the girl shiver.

☽ "How very noble and brave of you. There," she said, pointing, "there is your prince! And there he shall always be. And for your audacity in coming here, you shall soon join him!"

☽ The girl looked among the frozen animals and then, to her great horror and pain, she saw the figure of the great white bear who was her prince, frozen among them. The queen snickered and tossed a bundle at the young girl's feet.

☽ "Take this," she said. "It will remind you of the broken promise that sealed his fate."

☽ The girl picked up the bundle. It was the prince's white silken shirt with the three spots of tallow she had dripped on it.

At once, the girl began to cry. She cried for her prince, and for her broken promise to him, and for all the harm it had caused. Her tears fell on the shirt and touched the spots of tallow. But no sooner did the warm tears touch the wax than the spots began to melt. "Ahhh!" cried the queen. "What is happening? What are you doing?"  As the spots of tallow melted, so did the ice surrounding all the creatures frozen throughout the great hall. And then, right before the girl's eyes, all of the melting figures were transformed into people. "You horrid creature! What have you done?" The freed prince stepped forward, facing the queen. "She brought a magic that is far more powerful than your evil could ever be. It is the magic that comes from love."

On hearing this, the queen became hysterical and boiled with rage. Her disguise melted away and revealed her as she truly was, a horrid little troll. Then, in her fury, she spun around and exploded in a cloud of black smoke, never to be seen again. ☽ All of the people in the hall shouted for joy at their freedom, and the

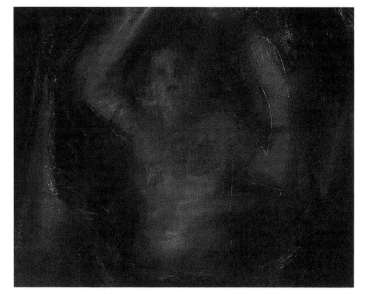

prince ran to the young girl. The prince then asked her what her greatest wish in the world might be, and without hesitation, she replied that she wished more than anything to be with him forever. And so it was. ☽ The North Wind came and swept them up and carried them far, far away from the castle that lay east of the sun and west of the moon.